My Ratchet Secret 3

Pebbles Vs Peyton

D1506385

No Where To Turn

This was it, the day that I dreaded with everything in my being. I hated asking anybody to do shit for me but I didn't have a choice. I had come to terms with the fact that not only did I have to kill Fallyn, but that I might not get away so easily this time. Hell I might not get away with it at all for that matter. The simple fact that someone saw me when I thought I had covered all my tracks the first time was a blatant reminder.

I hoped for the best but I had no choice but to prepare for the worse. If the shit hit the fan I had a backup plan. The only problem was that I needed money to fuel that plan. And what I had saved up just wasn't enough. If I needed to get away in a hurry there would be no time for making a pit stop at the bank to clean out the account. Not only that, if I started funneling too much too soon Adrian would become suspicious.

Aside from the fact that I needed something lethal and quick to take this bitch out, most likely a drug that would also paralyze her ass. I needed another ride that would serve as my getaway car, money to travel and supplies for the baby. Oh what? Y'all bitches think I ain't taking my baby with me? If this shit goes sour you can best believe I'm busting a move with the quickness and my damn baby will be by my side. There's nothing like a mother's love and I ain't leaving my kid with nobody.

As much verbal abuse as I put up with Fallyn's punk ass to get this little crumb snatcher, watching my man rubbing his hands all over this hoe's belly, and I CAN NOT forget that bitch maced me AND tried to blackmail me! Shiiiiittt…my baby WILL be with me no matter what.

The worst case scenario would me being on the run with a newborn but I had no choice but to get prepared. I know that's some ratchet shit to think about but fuck it, I had come too far to stop now. I had played it cool for as long as I could but the walls were closing in on my ass more each day. I had no choice but to pay a visit to the one person who could possibly help me. Someone I trusted and wouldn't ask any questions; that person was the Doc.

I pulled up to his office not knowing if he would even see me, let alone help me. I know that I broke his heart that night in the car when I told him that I couldn't be his woman but what was I supposed to do? I'm in love with my husband. Plus I already felt like he had the upper hand on me with knowing that I had once been a man and Adrian didn't have a clue. Not to mention the fact that he set me up with the egg donor and with Fallyn's crazy ass. Hell, he actually should be paying me seeing as she's the reason I'm going through all this bullshit in the first place.

Truth be told though, he could have exposed my secret long ago to Adrian but he didn't; even though he wanted me for himself. This told me a lot about his character. Even though he was bat shit crazy with that damn hand fetish of his, and he dressed like somebodies uncle that had escape from the damn nut house he was still crazy about me and that counted for something.

Aside from Adrian I didn't have anyone that I could count on or trust. And don't get the shit twisted, despite his tacky ass wigs and outfits, he was loaded. There was no getting around it, the Doc was my man. My only hope was that his ass wasn't going to want to cut another damn deal. I didn't want to fuck with him the long way but I had no choice. I don't know how much more of his freaky ass I can take.

None the less I needed him and whatever he wanted in return for the favor that he hopefully would be doing for me today I had no choice but to oblige seeing as he had the upper hand. Hopefully these two new wiglets that I picked up for him will help seal the deal. The rugs he had been wearing on his head made him look like a damn Muppet. His crazy ass needed to just let that shit go, but since he was hell bent on wearing a toupee I had my girl Soon Lee custom order him a few pieces.

"Damn baby to what do I owe this surprise?" the doc asked as he opened the door to his office.

"I need to talk to you about something important," I replied as I walked in and handed him the bag with the wiglets. "Here's a little present for you."

"Aww thanks paws I mean Pebbles. Have a seat."

"Please don't start with the names today Doc" I scowled, giving him the side eye.

He could barely wait till he sat down before tearing into the bag.

"Now lemme see what my baby done got for me."

Once he pulled out the wiglets he was beyond geeked, which was cool because I thought he might get offended at the idea of me picking out hair for him.

"Hot damn! You know what I like don't you tentacles?"

"Doc! The names!" I yelled. I was already antsy and anxious about even coming here to ask him for this huge ass favor and he wasn't making the shit any easier.

"Pebbles I'm sorry baby. I couldn't help it, I'm excited. I mean shit, it's not every day that brotha' like me gets gifts, usually somebody coming to me looking for a damn hand out. And here you done showed up with some new hair. I see you the type of woman that likes to dress her man. Is this want you wanted to see me in? Is this how you want ya man to look?" he asked as he paraded around the office with one of the new wiglets on top of the old one.

I hung my head in shame as the tears began to fill my eyes. The Doc was so engrossed with his new hair that it took a minute for him to realize that I wasn't responding to any of his comments.

When he finally took notice of my disdain he stopped what he was doing and took a seat at his desk.

"Paws... I mean Pebbles what is it baby?"

"I hated coming here to even bother you with this, especially since you say that everyone that stops by wants something from you. I'm ashamed to say that I'm one of those people.

As I wiped a tear away the Doc reach across the desk and took hold of my hand.

"Wassup baby? Talk to me...."

The look on the doc's face said it all. Just as I suspected he was clearly concerned with my wellbeing. The question was, just how much? Whatever sympathy I could get from him I had better take full advantage of considering I didn't know when I would be seeing him again.

"I don't know how to say this so I'm gonna just come right out and say it. I need a huge favor from you Doc.

The Doc's eyes grew large and a smile spread across his face. "You getting some booty injections girl? Not that I think you need them, but you can't never have too much junk in the trunk!"

"No! Just calm down and listen! Now I won't fault you if you say no but I really hope you say yes. I know I made fun of your wiglets and I know you don't….."

The Doc immediately became defensive and cut me off. "Who the hell wearing a wig? I don't wear no damn wigs. They're called scalp enhancements!"

"I'm sorry, your scalp enhancements…. I'm sorry I made fun of them, and I know I turned you down when you asked me to be your woman, but the thing is I'm with Adrian and…"

"Pebbles cut to the chase, tell me what you need."

The Doc was growing impatient with my stalling so I had no choice but to lay it all out on the line. Oh well here goes nothing.

"I need money and medical supplies. Now before you say no just hear me out. I plan on paying you back every dime that you let me hold." My voice shook as I spoke, not because I was nervous about asking him for the favor, but because I didn't want to hear no. If the Doc didn't agree to give me what I needed I had nowhere else to turn. It would call for drastic measures to be taken. I mean I'm a lady and all but I ain't above setting it off if need be.

By now the look of concern and confusion painted the Doc's face.

"How much money do you need baby? You know I got you but are you in some kind of trouble?"

"Sigh…. I need at least $20,000. I know that's a lot of money but I promise I will pay you back.

The Doc's mouth dropped open after hearing my request. I could tell he wanted to say "hell naw" but my eyes pleaded with him to say yes.

"Damn girl that's a lot of money. What you trying to do? Get them hands worked on? I told you I like them just the way they are" he said shooting a glance at my knuckles and blowing a kiss at them.

"No Doc, it's not the hands. I can't tell you what the money is for but I'm just asking that you please trust me on this. Here you can take my wedding ring as collateral and anything else valuable I can get my hands on."

The Doc noticed just how desperate I was by the way I was frantically trying to remove the ring from my finger as the tears once again began to fall.

"Hold up baby girl. As bad as I want you for myself I can't ask you to do that. You know I would love nothing more than for you to take that nigga's ring off and replace it with mine, but I don't want it under these conditions. I can tell that you must really need this loot bad."

"I do Doc, you know I wouldn't be coming here like this but I'm in a bind and I have nowhere else to turn. And for the record I realize I have to pay it back with interest."

I hung my head in disgust and defeat and spoke softly. "Just tell me what I have to do and I'll do it."

It was at that very moment I realized our relationship had taken a turn. I had not only become friends with the Doc, I saw just how much he really cared about me.

"Pebbles my feeling for you run deep girl. I wasn't lying about the shit I was saying to you in the car that night. I really do have love for you. You done brought joy to my life girl.

It ain't too many real women out here in the game and when I ran across you … well you opened up a niggas heart, made him feel like he can love again. That shit is priceless to me. Imma loan you the money and you ain't got to do shit. And you can pay me back whenever you can. I know you good for it."

"Thank you so much Doc." I beamed as I jumped up and threw my arms around his neck. "You don't know how much this means to me." Just as I suspected he had my back.

"Aww girl it ain't nothing, now about them medical supplies. What you looking to get? I hope it ain't no drugs. You know I could lose my license over some shit like that."

We both busted out laughing at statement, knowing full well that he did enough shit on a daily basis that would have BEEN cost him his license. The question was would he be willing to take a risk with me?

I had already researched the drug that I needed access to. It was called Vecuronium, a neuromuscular blocking agent that would paralyze a person. The only problem is it also stops their breathing as well. So that means the person must be ventilated or they will die in a matter of minutes. It was just the drug I needed for Fallyn's bitch ass. Oh yes I had some epic shit planned for that trick and I wanted her to feel every bit of it what I was about to put down without being able to move.

At this point the Doc was actually looking at me like I was crazy but he didn't ask any questions. As a matter of fact he said he didn't even want to know what I was using it for. At the end of the day each and every one of my requests were met. I left his office that day with a cashier's check that he popped out to get, the drugs as well as scrubs, masks, and surgical instruments that I lifted and put in my trunk when he stepped out to go get the check.

Like Ice Cube said "Today was a good day." Things were starting to look up for ole Pebbles. The Doc had made me truly happy. This was cause for a celebration. I was so damn happy when I saw that check in the Doc's hand that I snatched his shirt open and rubbed my hands all over his chest and belly, causing him to shudder and cum in under a minute.

"Why you do me like this hoofy? He panted as his knees buckled from the sensations that over took his body.

I left him standing in his office, a quivering, twitching mess as he tried to regain his composure and clean himself up. My work was done here, time for phase two.

Pebbles Verses Peyton

Now that I had the cash that I needed it was time to do some shopping. Over the course of the next few days I not only bought a used car and paid for it with cash, I found a secluded wooded area in an upper rural county, far away from our home to stash it. This would be my go to spot in case of emergency. My plan was to pack everything I needed for the road for myself and the baby. A bitch like me has to stay two steps ahead of everyone else at all times. I had slipped up once before so I had to be extra careful this go round. I had to make sure my shit was trump tight. If all goes well Adrian and I will be proud parents and Fallyn will be a nonfactor, allowing us to get on with our lives. However if the shit went sour I wanted to be fully prepared in case I had to jump ship.

Today was the day I planned on stopping by Wal-Mart to grab the items I needed like diapers and formula as well as a few gas cans. I had to be prepared just in case I was passing through a town where I could be spotted and couldn't stop for gas.

Before I got my journey underway I decided to make a detour at the mall. Fuck it, if imma be on the run who knows when I would get to go shopping again. My ass could very well be in hiding for the next damn year. I'm taking some of this money the Doc gave me and making sure my baby is fly as hell. That's right bitches, y'all though I was gon' be one of them mommas having their child look any kind of way? Hell naw! Pebbles don't roll like that. That rugrat is 'bout to be a reflection of me.

"Now lemme take my ass in here and see how much they want for these Jordan's," I said as I entered Kid's Foot Locker.

"Excuse me, can I get some help up in here" I yelled across the room to the clerk gossiping behind the counter with her coworkers. I wanted to tell her ass that she needed to be on this side of the counter, greeting customers but I decided to chill because I didn't want to get my pressure up. These young kids ain't got no kind of damn work ethic now a days.

"Welcome to Foot locker, can I help you?"

As if I wasn't already annoyed enough this little bird had the nerve to be standing up in somebody's place of business working with the damn lace showing on her wig, chipped up nails, and popping gum.

"Doze is on sale for $129.00," she said glancing at the shoe in my hand.

No this heffa ain't patting her shit like it's time for a touch up. I swear when my ass gets settled I might have to start a charm school to teach these chicks a thing or two about being a lady. This was expensive for a pair of shoes for a baby but fuck it. I got the cash and I want my child look good.

"I'll take a pair in the smallest size you have. See what other colors you have them in also."

"Ok ma'am I'll be right back."

"Ma'am? Ugh!! I DO NOT look like a ma'am!" I thought. Just because I'm 'bout to be somebody's momma don't mean that I actually look like one. I started to call her manager but I didn't want to get her little ass in trouble, plus I had to check myself and realize that everyone wasn't going to be like me. These little birds came a dime a dozen but I was a class act. True class was hard to find now a days. I was like a rare gem. Instead of responding I just smiled and nodded.

No sooner than she walked away I heard a man's voice.

"You ain't got room to be talking shit about nobody, with yo' crazy ass!"

I spun around to see who it was but no one was there.

"Look at yo' dumb ass buying all that expensive shit for a damn newborn. You need to be worried about stocking up on supplies but instead you trying to floss! It ain't like the baby gon' walk in the damn shoes."

I immediately became nauseas, who the fuck was this? I spun around looking from side to side but no one seemed to be talking to me. The store was quite busy but everyone was holding a conversation with someone else. I ran to the entrance to see if I could spot someone I recognized leaving. After I didn't see anyone I frantically began looking under clothes racks and behind displays. Somebody HAD to be fucking with me.

"Who the hell is that?" I yelled.

The man laughed, "Who the hell do you think it is? It's Peyton."

"Yous a lie! Show yourself!" I yelled.

"Uhmm you might wanna stop yelling before they kick yo' ass outta here."

I was just about to answer when I noticed that everyone in the store had now turned their attention to me! Not only was everyone looking at me like I was a damn nut job, the clerk had returned and was standing there with her mouth open.

"What the fuck? I must have damn turrets or some shit," I thought. The man's voice I heard was mine. I was talking to my damn self and everyone had heard me! I was humiliated.

"Ma'am," the clerk said with her voice shaking. "You still want deeze shoes?"

"Naw she don't want them, Pebbles take yo' ass home. You done made a damn fool of yourself" Peyton responded.

This time I paid attention and I actually felt my lips moving when he was talking! Tears flooded my eyes as I covered my mouth and fled from the store. When I finally got to the car I tried to pull myself together enough to drive. I couldn't understand was happening to me. All I knew was that I was losing it. As if I didn't have enough on my plate to deal with already, I was being possessed by Peyton!

I had heard about people with split personality disorders but who knew I would develop the shit myself? "You stronger than this girl" I said to myself as I wiped my tears away and drove off. "You can fight this shit. I didn't have time to be on no schizophrenic bullshit."

"That's what you think, you tried to kill me bitch but I'm here to stay."

"Fuck you Peyton! I left your ass in Korea!"

"I can't believe this shit," I sobbed. "This has got to be a side effect of some of them damn hormones." I had totally lost control. If it were someone else trying to cause me grief I could handle the situation, but that was just it. There was no one to "handle." I was talking to myself. My former self had come back to haunt me.

"Ain't no damn hormones. You done just lost yo' damn mind," Peyton blurted out in a deep raspy tone. It was amazing just how much my voice changed when he spoke. "You done did some abominable shit and it's coming home to roost."

"Shut up Peyton!"

I couldn't believe that I was actually having an argument with myself! And to make matters worse the shit got so heated that I actually had to pull over to the side of the road. I watched as the people in other vehicles pointed and gave me strange looks as they passed by. I could not believe that this was happening to me. What the hell else could go wrong?

I quickly went straight home. There was no time to make any other stops seeing as I might "turn" at any moment. I had to get a handle on this shit. There was no way I could let Fallyn see me like this, luckily for me she was napping when I got in. And what would be even worse was if Adrian saw me in that state.

How the hell would I explain some shit like this to him?

I decided to have a cocktail and fired up a blunt to help me relax before he got home. This had been an exhausting day. After I showered I slipped into some sexy yoga pants and a beater that showed off my nipple bar piercings. I then sprayed on my love potion from Victoria's Secret, Adrian loved that shit. No matter how my day went I always made sure I looked good when my man got home from work. I was a little tipsy by now but that didn't stop me from restyling my hair and applying fresh makeup.

After taking another toke off the blunt I looked in the mirror. Behold! It was not one but two reflections staring back at me, my current self as Pebbles and my former self as a man, Peyton. One thing that I couldn't deny was the fact that my parents don't make no ugly kids. I was still fine as hell as a man. I had chiseled features and a strong jaw bone that would knock any woman to her knees. I just couldn't understand why this muthafucka decided to show up now.

If it was one thing that I had learned from this whole ordeal was that everything was mind over matter. I would simply have to ignore this bastard till he went away. I mean hell I was feeling like the damn Ghetto Boys when they sang "My mind is playing tricks on me."

One thing that was for certain I had totally destroyed Peyton in the physical sense. The only thing that was left was to get rid of his spirit. I was every bit of a woman as far as I was concerned, inside and out. From my curvaceous hips to my full sexy lips that I was about to apply my Channel gloss over. However for some reason the manly side of me was trying to creep back in, I for damn sure couldn't let that happen. And the kicker was he appeared to be manlier than ever. Hell if I would have been this masculine before there wouldn't have been any need for a sex change.

As I applied the gloss to my lips Peyton began to speak.

"What the hell is that on your damn lips? Take that shit off."

Now that I was fully aware of the fact that I was talking to myself I decided not to answer this time. Instead I ignored the voice and proceeded with my beauty routine.

"Look at you… just look at what you done to me. Done changed up my body and shit. Wearing all that damn makeup, and them fake ass titties. That shit don't make you a damn woman. You ain't got no fucking uterus."

That was the straw that broke the camel's back. 'Fuck you, go away!" I yelled.

"I ain't going nowhere I'm here to stay. Bitches always tryin' to keep a nigga down. Well I got news for yo' ass Pebbles, yous a nigga!"

"Go to hell Peyton! I will not let you destroy me. I killed you!"

This bastard was persistent! I began flinging my body against the walls to try and rid myself of him. If I could have choked myself I would have.

"Get the fuck out of me" I grunted as a punched myself in the stomach causing me to dry heave.

"What the hell is that?" Adrian asked himself as he walked in the front door and heard the commotion coming from the master suite. He had gotten home early from work and it sounded like Pebbles was arguing with someone in the bedroom.

"You don't run me bitch," Peyton raged.

"What the fuck? That's a man's voice!" Adrian fumed as he made his way closer to the room before trying unsuccessfully to bust in. "Pebbles? Who is that in there with you? Open this damn door."

Oh shit! Adrian was home! What the hell was I going to do now? I looked around the room at the mess I had made from flailing myself around. I quickly tried to compose myself before opening the door. Thank God I had locked it when I got in.

"Pebbles open this damn door!" Adrian yelled as he beat on the door, threating to kick it in.

I opened it calmly and asked him what was wrong.

"Hey bae, how was your day? What are you out here yelling about?"

"Don't try that shit with me Pebbles, you got a man up in my damn house?"

"A man?" I laughed to try and play it off but the shit had hit the fan. "What are you talking about?"

"I ain't crazy; I heard a man's voice coming from this room. It sounded like y'all were arguing. Where is this nigga at? He bold enough to come up in here I'm fucking him up on contact."

He then proceeded to look under the bed, in the walk in closet and behind the shower curtains that he raked back so hard he almost tore down.

"Calm down! What you heard was the TV, I just turned it off." I was lying through my teeth and I prayed he believed me.

Adrian paced the floor looking around the room. I know it's a nigga in here, If not he just left," he grimaced as he looked out the window.

"Baby I swear it was the TV. I would never cheat on you."

Adrian walked over to the TV and felt it. "Then why ain't the shit warm?" He turned it on and the home shopping channel popped up. "It's a woman on this damn screen, you mean to tell me you were arguing with this woman on the TV?" He glared at me suspiciously. "And why was that damn door locked?"

"Because I was getting dressed ok? Damn I'm trying to tell you truth but that ain't good enough."

"Hell naw it ain't good enough, not after what my ears heard. Don't walk away from me woman!" He yelled as he snatched my arm to pull me back as I tried to brush past him.

"Nigga don't you ever put yo' damn hands on me!" Peyton yelled and body slammed Adrian into the dresser. He lay there shocked stunned at my sheer manly strength. Not to mention that fact that he couldn't believe that I had put hands on him.

Adrian could not believe what had just transpired. Not only did he suspect his beloved Pebbles of cheating on him; he had experienced a side of her that he had never seen before. Yes he was wrong for grabbing her arm but this woman had lost her damn mind! She had slammed his ass into the dresser like a rag doll. He had no idea that she was that strong. And the kicker was that when he looked at her afterwards she had certain hardness to her face that he hadn't noticed before. It was as if someone else had taken over her body.

I ran out of the room crying and locked myself in the car and wept. What had I done? I had hurt the one person who truly loved me. I prayed that he wouldn't leave me behind this stunt. Something had to be done to stop Peyton from creeping out. I couldn't let this shit ruin my marriage. I had put in too much damn work for that to happen.

After sitting in the car for over an hour I came to the realization that Adrian wasn't coming to be by my side. Usually it kills him to see me shed a tear. Any other time he would have been in this car with the quickness, trying to see what the problem was. I had really fucked up this time. Not only did I hurt him physically, I bruised his ego as well. I decided to go in the house and clean up the mess

Peyton had made of everything. I had to convince Adrian that I wasn't cheating on him and that he was the only man I loved. Once I apologized I know everything would be alright.

Upon entering our bedroom I looked around at the mess that was made when Peyton slammed Adrian. I began to pick up the pieces of the shattered cologne bottles before finally grabbing the broom. On the way to the kitchen I spotted Adrian in the bathroom wiping his face with wet washcloth. The look on his face spoke volumes. He had the look of pain and resentment in his eyes as my glance met his in the mirror. I immediately walked over to him and tried to touch his shoulder but he snatched away from me.

"Baby I'm so sorry, you just caught me off guard. I swear there wasn't man up in here. I would never cheat on you baby." I pleaded, hoping he would at least hear what I had to say.

Instead he pushed past me as if I was there and headed down the hall.

"Adrian, please just listen to me."

Before I knew it he quickly spun around and grimmed me like he was looking through me. I had never seen him look at me that way and I didn't like it one bit.

"Lemme tell you something," he scowled. "I was wrong for grabbing your arm but that shit you did in there was uncalled for. If I had of done some shit like that to you the fucking police would be here right now. My momma raised me not to hit women. Lucky for you cause yo' ass almost caught a damn beat down. I will tell you this though, that was your first and last time trying some shit like that with me. From now on imma keep my hands to myself but just know that if you decide to boss up like a nigga again imma beat yo' ass like a nigga!"

His eyes pierced through me like I was transparent. I had never seen him this pissed, He was literally seething.

"And for the record I know what the fuck heard. I just can't prove the shit. But it's all good, yo' ass will slip up again, and when you do its over."

With that he walked away and left me standing there with a lump in my throat. He REALLY did think I was cheating on him. How could he? As good as I have been to this man, this is what he accuses me of?

I knew that he would eventually come around like he always did. I just needed to give him his space and put some of this good loving on him. Yep that's would I would do. I'll throw this pussy so good on his ass tonight he won't know what hit him.

That night after Adrian went to bed I stayed up and put on one of my hoe outfits and strutted across the room. I was dressed in all white, like an angel. I had on white crotchless panties, white nipple tassels, and white thigh highs trimmed in white lace. There was no way Adrian would be able to resist me.

I couldn't have been more mistaken; he took one look at me and rolled his eyes in disgust. It was clear that he was just trying to play hard to get. All I needed to do was move in so he could get a closer look at this voluptuous ass and it would be a wrap.

"No this nigga ain't trying to reject my fine ass," I thought as I noticed him closing his eyes and folding his hands across his chest like he was going to sleep.

I crawled in the bed with him and tried to straddle him but he pushed me off of him and turned his back to me.

"Baby, I said I'm sorry..."

I tried to snuggle up next to him but he scooted further away from me and tucked himself in the covers so I couldn't touch him.

"Hug up next to that nigga you was talking to," he snapped.

It was useless; I had finally turned my baby against me. If I lose Adrian behind this bullshit I don't know what I will do. He was the only man I ever truly loved and now I feared that he was falling out of love with me.

After I turned out the lamp on my side of the bed I began to cry myself to sleep. What started out as a soft feminine whimper slowly morphed into the ugliest manly howl I had ever heard.

"Uhhhhh!! Uhhhhh!"

"*No Peyton ass wasn't crying,*" I thought.

"*Men cry too bitch,*" he responded in my mind.

I had to catch myself to keep from answering aloud. Just then Adrian rose up and turned around to see me ugly crying with enough base to shake the walls. He just shook his head and turned back over.

Suddenly there was a knock at the door, it was Fallyn. We had woke this bitch up.

"Y'all alright?"

"Yea' we cool," Adrian responded.

"Ok 'cause I heard all the commotion… I thought I just heard a coyote up in there."

Adrian turned and looked at me again.

"Yea' so did I…." he grunted.

This caused me to cry even harder. I covered my mouth, turned my back and put my head under the comforter till I dozed off. My life was truly fucked up!

Bitter Sweet Passion

I had just gotten in from another tiring day at work. I stretched out across the bed and turned the station to **Hoodz Most Wanted,** talk about some ratchet fools being busted? What started out as a local TV show that showcased and brought down the US' most wanted criminals had now turned into a nationwide sensation over the years. They worked closely with the FBI and police to bring these thug muthafuckas to justice, so you know a bitch like me had to peep in on them every now and then to make sure my black ass wasn't on there.

I hoped I could catch a nod before Adrian got in. We still hadn't made up and it was killing me. I mean we were at least on speaking terms but it had been over two weeks since he had touched me. I had to use my dilators to keep my shit open seeing as this was a record for us. Me and my boo usually don't miss a night getting it in. I had tried everything from wearing sexy outfits to cooking his favorite meal but he wasn't having it. Nothing was working. I had never seen him hold a grudge this long and frankly it was getting old. I mean hell if the nigga didn't know that he was the only man for me by now he never would.

It was when I least expected it Adrian came around. I was totally caught off guard. As a matter of fact I had totally given up on seducing him. He must have gotten tired of beating his meat and came to his senses. I knew it would only be a matter of time before he wouldn't be able to resist my sexy ass.

As I slept in my usual position on my belly with one leg slightly raised higher I felt the caress of Adrian's strong hands kneading my ass. I smiled to myself as I felt his lips trace my shoulder. I knew it! I knew this nigga couldn't resist me! I turned my head back so that my lips met his for a sensuous kiss, his dick was rock hard pressing into my lower back.

I had to discreetly spit on my hand and slide it between my legs before he turned me over and entered me, seeing as I didn't have time to apply lube.

Adrian pounded me fast and hard, almost like his intention was more of getting his nut rather than trying to please me as he normally would. It was all good though. It had been so long since we had gotten it in that I was just happy to have my man on top of me. There was nothing for me to do except lay back and enjoy the ride.

I dug my nails into his back and nibbled on his ear lobe. Damn it felt sooooo good to have Adrian inside of me even if it was for his own satisfaction.

"Right there baby, that feels so good" I moaned softly as he stroked me deeply.

"Ohhhh shit!! Yeeah!!" I growled in a deep husky tone.

"*What the fuck?*" I thought to myself. Peyton's punk ass was trying to resurface at the worst possible moment! Not now, please not now!"

It was too late. The base in my voice had made Adrian's dick shrivel up like a Vienna sausage. Before I knew it had slid out of me and jumped up.

"What the hell was that?"

"What baby? What's wrong?" I asked trying to play the shit off knowing full well what had just went down.

"What the hell is wrong with your voice? You coming down with something?" Adrian responded with a look of confusion and disgust.

"It's nothing baby. I was just in the moment. You felt so good to me. Come back to bed daddy, lemme lay some of this good loving on you." I pleaded.

"Nah uhhh, that's alright, I'll pass." Adrian proceeded to slip on his pajama pants and hop on his side of the bed.

"Bae come on, don't let that stop you." I tried to touch him but he pulled away.

"My dick can't get hard with you sounding like James Earl Jones! You need to get that shit checked out. You might have a polyp or something on your damn windpipe."

"*What a complete asshole*" I thought. "There is nothing wrong with my damn windpipe Adrian," I responded with my voice shaking on the verge of tears.

"Well, all I know is that shit freaked me out. Fuck it I'm going to sleep."

I laid there once again humiliated as he turned his back to me. Peyton had messed up what was supposed to be a beautiful night of love making. I had to find a way to get this shit under control before I lost my man completely.

Dropping That Load

As if that night wasn't bad enough, to make matters worse I was tired as hell the rest of the week. And we had been up half the night last night with Fallyn. Her ass was having contractions so Adrian rushed her to the hospital only for it to be a false alarm. Well I wasn't having that shit tonight. If that bitch breaks my rest tonight it better be the real deal. Her ass is always being extra. She could have waited that shit out a while longer but noooo she just had to have all the attention on her. She was already on my shit list. I had a half of mind to cuss her ass out for that damn coyote remark she made the other night.

"Damn these contractions are kicking my ass!" Fallyn thought to herself as she rubbed her huge tight belly.

She had just finished eating and had stretched out in the family room to watch her afternoon lineup. She was trying her best to ignore the sharp pains that pulsated through her abdomen seeing as her OB GYN had sent her back home last night telling her that she hadn't dilated enough.

"Ouch!"

Fallyn winced in pain as she attempted to get up and go in her room lie in her own bed. As soon as she turned the corner in the hallway she caught another pain that caused her knees to buckle.

"Oh shit!"

She looked down to see gush of liquid that had flowed from between her legs and was now running down her thighs. Her water had broken. She used her hand to brace herself against the doorframe and called for help.

"Help me!" Fallyn called out.

I popped my eyes open from what was about to be a perfect afternoon nap to hear Fallyn moaning and squealing in the hallway.

"Whaaaatt? Damn!" I yelled from my room. I had just laid my ass down and I wasn't about to get up.

"Help me dammit! I'm in labor!"

"Aww shit here we go with this shit again." I jumped up mad as hell and stormed out of the bedroom and down the hall. I was just about to tell this bitch to get her life when she screamed out again.

"Hurry up! My water broke!" she cried.

I totally ignored that shit she was talking when I looked down and saw the huge pink wet spot on my damn white carpet. "I know you didn't just fuck up my carpet?"

"I'm having the baby dumb ass! Is that all you can worry about is your damn carpet?"

I was about to grab the cleaning solution for the rug and have that heffa spot clean it until I looked at her face. She was clearly in distress. "*Maybe she is having the baby for real this time,*" I thought.

"So you for real this time?" I asked looking her writhing body up and down.

"I was for real the last time! AHH!! SHIT!!" Fallyn bent over and grasped her belly. What were sharp twinges had now turned into full-fledged contractions. "I need to get to the hospital before I have this baby right here, lemme call Adrian."

I had to think quickly. If she really was having the baby I didn't want her calling anyone. I'm the head bitch in charge and I would see that she got to the hospital.

"Ok Ok….. lemme help you to the car." I attempted to put my arm around her but she started flailing her arms frantically.

"Noooo get your hands off of me! I want Adrian!"

"*I know you do bitch,*" I thought to myself.

Fallyn made a final attempt to make it to her room to grab her cell phone but her knees failed her and started to buckle again. Just as she was about to fall I threw my arms around her waist and started dragging her towards the front door.

"Look at you, you can't even walk."

"Stop it! Somebody help me!" Fallyn swung and struck me cutting my top lip.

"You betta' settle yo' ass down! I'm trying to help you bitch; now stop fighting me and get yo' ass in this car!" I sneered.

Fallyn wanted to continue to fight but it was useless, she was too weak. And the contractions were now five minutes apart.

"What about my bag? And we need to call Adrian!" she protested as I shoved her into the car.

"No time for that I'll come back for it."

There was time but I wasn't trying to hear that shit she was talking. Not only was I going to be the one to call Adrian. I didn't want her to have her bag till I got a chance to snoop through it first. Ain't no telling what her sneaky ass might be up to.

"Yo' crazy ass betta' take me straight to the hospital or I swear….."

"You swear what? All you need to be worrying about is not messing up my damn seats. Close yo' damn legs!" I snapped as I tasted the blood from my top lip.

"Unbelievable! I'm having a….. baby and all you can think about is material shit, you shellfish bitch! That's how I know yo' twisted ass…. don't need a child."

"Don't piss me off Fallyn! Shut yo' ass up and ride! I love that baby, imma make a good momma," I said glancing at her belly.

"Please… you don't….. know the meaning…… of the word love…. you selfish and hateful."

Fallyn had started breathing heavy, heaving and gasping between her words.

"That's…. why yo' ass going crazy. I be hearing you…… in there talking to yo' self, sound like a man. Who…. is it Peyton? I hope his ass…… don't come out while you driving. You done…. already pushed Adrian away…. crying like Barry White. Yo' ass…. was howling like… you was on Twilight, scared… the shit outta me. I had to… make sure… Adrian was alright."

The bitch tried to laugh but instead she was hit with another pain.

I cut my eyes at that hoe. "That's what yo' ass gets. Keep talking shit and yo' ass gon' end up in the trauma center when we get here instead of labor and delivery."

She was trying her best to rustle my feathers but I paid her no attention. I was on a mission to let her have this baby so I could move on to the next phase of my plan. As we approached the hospital I called Adrian to let him know that Fallyn was in labor. Then I quickly swooped into the spot in front of the emergency entrance for expecting mothers, jumped out and grabbed a wheel chair.

Before we knew it several nurses had come to assist us. They moved quickly to process Fallyn then whisked her away to a delivery room. Shortly after I met up with Adrian as he emerged from the elevator.

"Where is she? Is everything ok?" he asked, searching for the room Fallyn was in.

"She's fine; they are getting her hooked up so they can monitor her contractions."

"Why didn't you guys call me sooner? I would have dropped what I was doing and come straight home."

"I know you would have baby, but there was no time."

"Mr. and Mrs. Ramsey?"

"Yes that's us" Adrian responded.

"Hello I'm Dr. Branford. I will be assisting with the birth today. Will either of you being joining us in the delivery room?"

"I will," Adrian quickly responded. "Bae are you coming?"

"Naw… you go on. That type of stuff makes me squeamish."

"If you would please follow me Mr. Ramsey we will get you scrubbed up and draped. The waiting room is around the corner to your left Mrs. Ramsey."

"Thank you Dr."

I gave Adrian a quick peck on his lips and sent them on their way. There was no way I wanted to be looking up this bitch's ass while she was having that baby. I already felt some kind of way about the fact that it wasn't me lying there on that table having Adrian's child. Hell if I had a choice in the matter he wouldn't be in there either, looking at some other woman's pussy. It didn't matter though, that would be his first and last look. As soon as this trick drops this load it's over for her ass.

I paced the floor and waited for the news. Dr. Branford finally arrived in the lobby after only an hour and a half to tell me that we had a healthy baby boy!

I raced into the room to see Adrian beaming with pride at his new son. And I could totally understand why, he was absolutely beautiful! I have to admit when he started talking shit about wanting a baby I wasn't really trying to hear it. In fact it was the furthest thing from my mind. But after seeing our little bundle of joy I immediately fell in love! His face was almost cherubic, with his little chubby cheeks. And he had a head full of cottony black hair. My baby was a little butter ball, weighing in at 8lbs and 3ozs.

"He's beautiful" I gushed as I held my son in my arms.

"Just like his momma," Adrian said softly as he kissed me on the forehead.

This was the first time he had shown me any tenderness since our failed attempt at making love. I should have known that this little angel would bring us back together. At the end of the day I knew Adrian really loved me and nothing could change that. We held each other and looked at the blessing God had given to us. We finally had our happy little family. This was truly a Hallmark moment, at least it was till that damn Fallyn started coming to her senses. The drugs were starting to wear off and she was becoming a bit more chipper.

"Stop touching his face," Fallyn hissed as she watched me caress little AJ's cheek. "Get them big rusty hands out of my baby's face."

My maternal instincts instantly clicked in and I was about to check this hoe with the quickness but my boo beat me to the punch.

"Your baby?" Adrian asked with the look of surprise on his face.

"I mean the baby… sorry I just got so attached to him in that short period of time."

"Humph…." I just smirked and ignored that hoe. It was killing her to see our family together. She thought she was going to be Adrian's jump off but little did she know we had a love that you don't find every day. And no amount of money could buy that. It would take a lot more than just a pretty face and a fat ass to grab my baby's attention.

"I can't wait to take you home little man" Adrian whispered over my shoulder to the baby.

His tiny hand was gripping my pinky finger so tight that I knew beyond a shadow of a doubt that he knew who his momma was. You couldn't have told me that I didn't lie down on that table and push him out myself the way we bonded.

"I can't wait either" I cooed as I kissed his hand.

"If you don't get them crusty soup coolers away from him I'll…."

"You'll what?" I asked with a docile tone to my voice. My interaction with the baby was obviously driving her ass crazy and I wasn't about to let Adrian see me get ugly. Not today, imma let this bitch show her true colors so he can see her for who she truly is.

"Fallyn! What's gotten into you?" Adrian snapped. "I understand you being protective but you going too far. That's my wife you talking about. If you want to hold the baby again just say so but let's not forget Pebbles is the child's mother."

And there it is. My baby had checked the shit out of her ass and I loved every minute of it.

Fallyn wanted nothing more than to show her natural black ass but she couldn't let Adrian see this side of her seeing as she had her own agenda.

"I'm so sorry; I don't know what came over me. It must be emotions. Yes I do want to hold him again."

"It's ok Fallyn. I totally understand, after all you did carry him for nine months," I said as I walked over to hand her the child. As I bent down to place him in her arms I discreetly whispered in her ear. "You heard my husband bitch, I'm his momma."

I smiled and stood back at the look of defeat on that bitch's face. This bird thought she was gonna take my man? She had the game all fucked up.

"Ohhh Adrian, I almost forgot I need my bag. I didn't get a chance to grab it." Fallyn grumbled, giving me the sideeye.

Before he could get a chance to answer I offered to go and get it.

"It's ok Pebbles I know you want to stay here with the baby," Fallyn responded.

You know the saying "game recognizes game?" well that's exactly what I was doing, peeping this hoe's game. The last thing she wanted was for me to get loose in her room and snoop around. Or better yet, seeing what she had in her little bag of tricks. For that very reason I made sure her ass didn't get a chance to get to it before we left for the hospital.

"Nahh… I need to get some air anyway. I'll be back in a few."

I quickly pulled out my car keys and headed towards the door before Adrian could offer to take over the task.

"You sure bae? I don't mind going."

"I insist, just sit right there and keep out son company till I get back."

The look on Fallyn's face was priceless. I had won again and she couldn't do shit about it. After giving Adrian a quick peck on the lips I headed for the car, but not before stopping off to the nurses' station to give strict orders for the baby to be placed on formula. Fallyn's ass was already talking bout she was attached to little AJ. I'll be damned if I was gonna let that wanch put her titty in my baby's mouth.

No Stone Unturned

Upon making my way back to the house I made a mad dash for Fallyn's room. I had to move quickly because I wanted to get an adequate amount of snooping in without staying gone too long. Plus I didn't want to leave Adrian alone with that bitch any longer than I had too, just in case she started running off at the mouth. At this point the only thing that was stopping her was the fact that she THOUGHT she was about to cash in.

First things first, I snatched open the bag that she had packed to take to the hospital. It was full of the usual toiletries, pajamas, and clothes.

"What's this?"

I pulled out what looked to be a smaller tote rolled up inside of her suitcase. Inside was an outfit for an infant boy along with a receiving blanket and a pair of booties. She was trying to sneak her own outfit in for the baby to wear home. This chick had truly lost her mind if she thought she was about to be dressing my baby. I knew her slick ass wanted this bag so bad for a reason. She got a lot of damn nerve trying to steal away my joy of motherhood. I already had little AJ's outfit picked out and she didn't have a damn hand in it.

"Lemme see what else is in here"

As I shuffled through her belongings I noticed a secret compartment in the bottom of the suit case under the lining.

"Well lookie what we have here"

I pulled back the lining and unzipped the compartment to reveal a can of mace.

I laughed out loud as I carefully placed the mace back in the compartment and put everything just as I had found it. It wasn't a surprise. I knew she had something up her sleeve. The funny part was the fact that she thought that a can of mace was all she needed to protect her from my wrath. Yeah she caught me off guard the first time but the bottom line was, when it was time for the shit to really hit the fan they gon' need a crowbar to pry me off of her ass.

Now it was time to check her room.

"I wonder can I find those damn pictures."

I yanked out each dresser drawer and shuffled through it before flipping her mattress up. I didn't find the pictures but I did find the daily journal she kept. It laid her plan to set me up from the jump. Not only that, she had chosen where she was going to get new furniture for the house once I was gone, and how she was going to decorate each room specifically. It also spelled where she and Adrian were getting married once he divorced me! She had little AJ's preschool picked out and everything!

"Humph! And the bitch wants to call me crazy?"

"You are crazy. In here going through her shit like a damn lunatic instead of having yo' ass at the hospital with that baby."

I totally ignored Peyton's ass. Now was not the time!

I quickly ran in the living room and hid the journal in the guest closet on the top shelf inside of an old purse. It was too much juicy shit up in there and I needed plenty of time to read it without any distractions. Plus if push came to shove I just might be able to use it as evidence in my defense if I needed to plead insanity for murking this hoe.

After the book was hidden I went back into Fallyn's room and began searching her closet then finally under her bed.

"Jackpot!"

I pulled out the locked metal box and shook it. I don't know what the hell was in there but it was heavy as hell. I ran to the kitchen to grab a flathead screwdriver from out of the toolbox we kept under the kitchen sink.

I could give a shit about busting the lock seeing as she wasn't making it back to this room anyway. As a matter of fact the clock was ticking down fast for Ms Fallyn. She wasn't stepping foot back into this house ever again if I had anything to do with it.

My eyes popped when I saw all the tricks she had in her basket. I had underestimated her. This bitch had Chinese stars, mace, hell she even had a damn gun! This heffa had enough weapons to take down a small army.

"Oh this hoe was gon' try and tase a bitch! Boy I'm so glad I followed my first mind and checked up on her ass," I said as I picked up the taser and examined it.

"Damn she was gon' fuck you up!"

"Shut the hell up Peyton! Can't you see I'm trying to handle business?"

I grabbed the suitcase and tossed it in the trunk then hid the box of weapons in the garage before heading back for to hospital. It was time to wind this story on down but first I need to make a final appearance to sit with the baby for a bit then bring Adrian back home and put him to bed. I had bigger plans for the night and I needed to get the ball rolling.

Nightmare On Pebble's Street

Crrreeeaaakk

The sound of the basement steps echoed in my ears as I ascended down into the dimly lit room to gather the clothing that I would be wearing for the night. I decided to dress in all black till I got to the location with my real disguise. I had already moved the toys I would be using to the car inside of a back pack. There would be no time for popping the trunk plus I didn't want to draw any attention to myself. I had already taken care of Adrian by adding an Ambien to the shot of Henny I fixed for him before we retired for the night.

After driving to the location where I had my getaway car parked I quickly changed into the scrubs I had lifted from the Doc's office and grabbed the surgical tools and placed them in my backpack. I then switched cars and drove to the hospital.

I moved swiftly past the nurses' station on the floor below Fallyn's so that I could drop the backpack with the supplies I needed into a laundry cart and cover it with sheets.

As the elevator reached the floor Fallyn was on my heart raced. I couldn't believe this was it. I was finally about to do it. The notion that I was now in fact a cold blooded murderer never came into play considering all that was at stake. Fallyn thought this shit was a game and it was, it time for me to show her that this shit was chess and not checkers.

My eyes darted around the long corridors searching for anyone or anything that may give me away. I was dressed as one of "them" so I blended in perfectly. I was also sure to slide up the surgical mask I wore to further distort my appearance from probing cameras. My only fear; I hoped that the baby was in the nursery so that he didn't have to witness what was about to go down.

Once the doors opened I headed straight to the room that I had previously cased earlier that day that had a ventilator. I would need it to keep Fallyn alive long enough to torment her after giving her the paralyzing shot. And as luck would have it, it was still there. I wanted to kiss that damn machine when I saw it but there was no time. Luckily I had already done my research and figured out how to work the thing from a few YouTube videos.

Basically all I would need to do is insert the breathing tube up her nose and down into her windpipe and turn the machine on. To hell with the settings seeing as this was about to be her lasts moments of life anyway. I was going to take great pleasure in doing this, seeing as under normal circumstances the procedure would be done with anesthesia. In Fallyn's case I would be sure to give her enough of the drug to stop her from fighting back or moving but not enough to totally deaden all sensations in her body. That wouldn't be any fun now would it?

I dropped off the laundry cart, hooked my backpack onto the side of the machine where it couldn't be seen and headed towards Fallyn's room.

The clock in the hallway read exactly 12:45. It was so late and slow on that unit that I could actually hear the nurse's staff gossiping, swapping stories about their husbands and kids. This was the perfect scenario in the fact that it allowed me slip right past them undetected.

Before entering Fallyn's room I paused and removed the syringe full of my parallelizing cocktail and removed the cap. I had to be ready to act fast just in case she was awake.

I slipped into her room like the grim reaper. As I stood by the doorway for a split second I scanned the room to see if the baby was there, which he wasn't, as well as to see if her eyes were open.

In a flash I pounced like a panther about to devour its prey. I covered her mouth in case she tried to scream and stabbed her in the neck with the syringe. Her eyes popped open just in time to feel the drug rushing through her veins as I mashed down the plunger.

Her weakened attempt to grab at my wrist was short lived as the lethal cocktail cursed its way through her blood stream. Her body went limp allowing only involuntary twitches from her paralyzed limbs and an occasional blink of an eye.

Once I saw that she couldn't move or scream I quickly locked the room door and went to work. The confused look that was frozen on that bitch's face was priceless. She had no idea know who or what had hit her.

I knew it would only be a matter of time before she would expire if I didn't make haste in hooking her ass up to the ventilator. I was gonna do it, but first I needed to show this skank exactly who was pulling on the puppet strings. I needed for her to see who stood between her hanging on to the last few miserable moments of life she had left before taking her last breath.

I damn near had an orgasm from the sheer exhilaration of standing over her and slowly pulling down my mask to reveal my identity. A single tear fell from her eye as I stared at her with a sinister grin before bending over and whispering in her ear as I used the end of the tubing to push the tip of her nose up to resemble a snout.

"I'm the puppet master tonight hoe."

She now fully understood what was about to happen.

As I briefly reveled in the moment I was snapped back into reality by her eyes rolling around in her head as she struggled to breath. Even though I knew she couldn't speak or move I knew that she could hear me.

"This is gonna hurt you a lot more than it hurts me."

With that I rammed the plastic tube up her nose. Her body jerked and convulsed as I shoved it past her nasal cavity and down into her throat before flipping the switch. She once again went limp as the life giving gas flooded her lungs.

"Damn she is a fine muthafucka. I know Adrian wanted to hit that bad as hell."

"Go straight to hell Peyton."

I moved her bed to a sitting position to prepare her for the show. And to make sure that she didn't miss anything I decided that I would whip out a few push pins to tack her eyelids open. We couldn't have those pesky things trying to blink now could we?

"Ms Fallyn Roberts, the chick who thought she was gon' run up and take Pebble's man and her baby? You do realize that you are a sick individual for even plotting some shit like that right?" I asked as I stood over her dangling the journal in front of her now bulging eyeballs.

"I have to give it to you; you had a pretty good scheme going. The only problem is you didn't realize who you was fucking with. You thought you knew me because I killed my best friend but what I'm about to do to you is gon' make her death look like child's play. You might as well call me Chucky tonight bitch."

"Remember when you told me to bow down? Uhh huhh well look whose back on top bitch! Me, Pebbles. Did you really think you could keep a good woman down? Did you really think that you could just waltz in and come between the love of a man and his wife? Better yet did you really think I would let you? I know you thought you had won but Pebbles always wins in the end. Didn't your momma ever tell you that God don't like people who act ugly? Well it's about time I made your face match that ugly ass heart of yours" I could clearly see the terror in Fallyn's eyes and it was absolutely invigorating.

I grabbed the scalpel from the back pack and proceeded to scalp the front half of Fallyn's head from ear to ear. Her eyes immediately went bloodshot and began to water as the blade tore through her flesh. Once the air her open scalp it felt like it was being hit with a blowtorch. I left her hairline looking like Naomi Campbell meets Stevie Wonder. I wanted to dance around her bed and do an Indian war cry while waiving that bitches scalp but there was no time.

"You thought you was a pretty bitch didn't you? Didn't you know it would take more than a pretty face to steal my boo away from me? Always trying to make cracks about how I look like man. Well the joke is on you now bitch."

"Make her ass look like the joker" Peyton laughed.

"That's the first thing you have actually said that made some sense. I think I might just do that."

I took the blade and sliced the corners of her mouth up into a smile. Before I knew it my rage had taken over and I sliced her lips completely off, exposing both rows of her teeth.

I was about to make an example out of her ass for anyone who dared stand in my way.

I looked down to see her exposed teeth clench and her tacked eyelids twitching from the pain.

"Let's see if Adrian wants your ass after this."

I then pulled out the bottle of acid she had in her box of tricks and splashed it onto her face and chest.

I giggled gleefully as her flesh burned down to the white meat.

Once I felt I had spent a sufficient amount of time torturing her I then turned off the ventilator, snatched out the tube and poured the remainder of the acid down her throat. When it was all said and done I left her there to suffocate from lack of oxygen and choke to death on her melting esophagus.

I peeked out of the window to her door to case the area before retracing my tracks and leaving exactly the way I had come in.

The night air was crisp as I drove back to the spot where I had switched cars. Once I was back in my normal clothes and heading home I let out a huge sigh of relief. It was finished. I had finally taken care of the only thing that stood between my family and our everlasting happiness.

Showtime

"What the hell? Are you serious? Is my child ok? We'll be right there!"

I heard the phone ring just moments before. I knew it was only going to be a matter of time before someone contacted us from the hospital about Fallyn's death. Adrian jumped to his feet and was in the process of getting dressed. It was once again time for one of my Oscar winning performances; hopefully this would be my last one. Now that I had told momma about the sex change and Fallyn was nonfactor there was nothing stopping me from finally having the family reunion I had always dreamt of. I had faith in my heart that they wouldn't share my secret with Adrian once they saw that I was truly happy.

"What's the matter bae?" I asked slowly lifting my head from the pillow.

"Fallyn is dead! We have to get to the hospital now! Get dressed!"

"What? Oh my God! What happened? Where's the baby? Is he ok?"

"I don't know what happened! The hospital ain't saying shit. All they said was there was an accident and Fallyn is dead. They assured me that the baby wasn't in the room, but you know I ain't trying to hear that shit. I'm going to get my son now!"

Adrian was literally tripping and falling as he frantically tried to get his feet into his pant legs. It was bad enough that the call had come at like 5:15 am and his alarm hadn't even gone off yet, he was still groggy from the drug I had given him earlier And although the news of Falynn's death totally caught him off guard I could tell his main concern was for our son, and rightly so. I mean at the end of the day let's not get it twisted; Fallyn's was just a uterus that was needed to carry our child. When it was all said and done nothing or no one could take the place of family.

I broke down into totally hysteria. I had to make the shit good and convincing.

"Oh my goodness, she was such a sweet girl. What could have happened to her?" I cried as I joined my husband getting dressed.

By now his clothes were on and he was about to run out the door with one shoe on his foot.

"I don't know but death keeps hitting close to home. I can't get past the death of Tasha before something like this happens. What the hell is the world coming too?"

The sadness in his eyes was a reflection of the pain of losing his sister. Somehow it always came back to this.

"Hurry up, I have to find out what kind of accident went down," Adrian yelled as he headed out of the front door to start the car.

"I'm right behind you."

The hospital was a scene of utter chaos, staff running about in all directions, News cameras. The police had whole unit basically on lock down. It was revealed to us once we got there that Fallyn had in fact been brutally murdered. The police were on a man hunt for her killer. Not only did they have the whole unit taped off for evidence. They called us in to identify the body.

After pushing past the nurses and police officers that were standing guard in front of the nursery we were finally able to see our son and hold him.

Adrian let out a sigh of relief as he stroked his hair. Before he knew it the tears began to flow.

"I don't know what I would have done if something would have happened to you lil man."

After a brief family moment I decided to go back in the hall and continue my performance.

"What kind of damn facility are you fucking running? Anybody can just walk in off the street? What if our son was in that room? I'm calling my attorney today!"

I ranted and raved till Adrian made his way to my side to calm me down.

"Calm down bae, we gon' get through this. At least the baby is ok. Now let's go view this body so we can get the hell out of here and put this nightmare behind us."

Before we got a chance to head to the morgue we were stopped by one of the detectives on the case.

"Mr. and Mrs. Ramsey?"

"Yea', who wants to know?" Adrian quipped. It was clearly evident that he was agitated.

"Hello I'm detective Frank Bridges. I was assigned to the case of Fallyn Roberts. Would you mind if I ask you and your wife a few questions?" he asked flipping open his badge before whipping out a notepad and pen.

Immediate panic set in as my knees began to tremble. I wondered what the hell he wanted with us. Could it be possible that he was on to me? I had to try my best to maintain my composure and not appear nervous.

"Yea' that's cool, what do you want to know?" Adrian responded.

"I just have a few routine questions. I promise that it won't take that long. If you like we can step into one of the conference rooms for more privacy."

"To be quite honest detective I'm ready to get this night over with and take my son home. Since you said it's not gonna take that long can we just answer the questions while we head down to the morgue?" asked Adrian as he headed towards the elevator.

"That's fine by me."

"So do they have any idea who would have done such a thing?" I chimed in to not only see if they had any leads. I was also trying to read the detective's eyes to see if in fact I was a suspect.

"Not yet ma'am. If you don't mind me asking how long have you known Ms. Roberts?"

"Almost a year," I responded.

"And how long had she been living with the two of you? It is just you and your wife living in the home correct?" He directed the question towards Adrian this time.

"Yes it's just the two of us. She moved in about three months ago."

"Have either of you heard her mention that she had any enemies?"

"Humph! Little did they know that bitch's number one enemy was me," I thought before answering.

"No I haven't heard her mention anyone, what about you bae?"

"Nah, Fallyn was sweet girl as far as I could see. I can't imagine her having any enemies."

"Did she mention getting into an argument with anyone?"

"No to me," Adrian shook his head. I followed suit with his answer.

"Do either one of you know of any reason someone would want her dead?"

I almost had to bit my damn tongue off to avoid blurting out the fact that she was a lowdown scandalous cunt that deserved everything that she had coming to her. Instead I just gave a weak smile and answered.

"No detective I'm sorry but she hasn't shared any incidents with me at least. That poor girl didn't have a mean bone in her body. She was like family to us."

"I'm cosigning with everything my wife had said." Adrian nodded his head in agreement."

"Great, that will be all for now. Here's my card if you can think of anything that might help. Don't hesitate to call me day or night. Is there a number you can be reached at?"

I quickly tried to offer my cell number but Adrian insisted that he give his. He must have read my mind because Lord knows if this man were to call back he damn sure wouldn't be getting an answer.

After speaking with the detective we continued on our journey to view Fallyn's body.

Adrian slid his arm around my waist and pulled me towards him as we descended down the hallway with two officers escorting us.

My stomach was literally quivering at the thought of viewing Fallyn's dead body. I knew

I had fucked her up pretty bad. And even though she had it coming to her, I was torn between seeing a vision that could possible haunt me the rest of my life verses the arrogant side of me that actually wanted to see my handy work.

What I couldn't understand was why they needed us. I mean didn't this bitch have a next of kin listed? I guess I really shouldn't complain. The less people on the scene the better until this whole thing blew over.

Before we entered the morgue one of the officers warned us that what we were about to witness was very graphic. He then went on to warn us of the injuries that were inflicted upon her.

"It was like a wild animal got to her" the officer explained

"Damn that sounds barbaric! Are you sure you want to go in bae? You can stay out here if you want to" Adrian asked.

I shook my head as I choked back the tears.

"No I'll go in with you. I don't want you to have to face this alone. Plus Fallyn was there for us when we needed her. We should be there for her."

With that we held hands as we slowly walk into the dank cold room. Fallyn's body lie flat of her back with her face completely mangled and her hairline gone.

I was almost tickled at the sight of that bitch's permanent grin. Needless to say I had to play the shit off in front of Adrian.

"DAMN! What kind of sick monster would do this to another human being?" Adrian recoiled at the site of Fallyn's mutilated face that was pink and still oozing from the acid. If it wasn't for her wrist band and dental records or the fact that the blood matched samples that had been taken from her previously no one would have ever known that it was her.

"Oh Lawd why they have to do her like this?" I screamed as I bolted out the room and proceeded to race up and down the halls. By the time Adrian and the officers caught up with me I had fell out in the middle of the waiting room floor balling.

"Not my Fallyn! Why they do her like this Lawd?"

"Baby its gon' be ok. Come on let's get you home." Adrian tried to pull me to my feet but I continued to kick and wail. You would have thought I was break dancing the way I spun around on that damn floor.

"Is she going to be ok? I can see if one of the doctor's will prescribe a sedative" one of the nurses asked out of concern.

"That might not be a bad idea" Adrian responded as he and the officer helped me up.

"*Aww shit, they bout to drug a bitch. Time to wrap this shit up and take this show on the road,*" I thought."

"Imma be ok," I sniffled.

"You sure bae, cause we can have them give you something to help you rest if you need it. I have a feeling it's about to be a rough day."

"No I'm good." I staggered to my feet and wiped my eyes. "As long as I have you and AJ I know I'll be ok."

"That's right, we gon' get through this as a family" Adrian reassured me as I laid my head on his shoulder.

"I know sweetie, I just want to get our baby and go home."

As we walked past the door to the morgue I couldn't help but notice the officers talking to a black guy that appeared to be in his early thirties. It appeared as though they were going to let him in to view the body as well. I had to think fast. I needed to know who this was and why the police called him.

Before I knew it I had switched directions and walked directly over to him. I wanted to catch him before he entered the room. Adrian looked a bit surprised but he followed right behind me out of curiosity.

"Excuse me are you related to Fallyn?"

"Yes I'm actually her fiancé. And you are?"

"I'm Pebbles and this is my husband Adrian. It's so nice to meet you. Fallyn never mentioned you."

Adrian and I were both shocked and surprised to say the least. Our emotions must have been painted across our faces judging by his response.

"Hey nice to meet both of you. I hate that it had to be under these circumstances. I'm Dorian."

He was choked up but managed to fight back the tears as he shook both of our hands.

"Nice to meet you bro', my wife is right, Fallyn never even mention she had a boyfriend let alone a fiancé," Adrian responded.

"*And a fine one at that,*" I thought as I examined his chocolate frame from head to toe. I have to admit that the bitch had good taste in men. I mean he didn't hold a candle to my boo but if I were single I would turn his sexy ass out just like I did Adrian. Now the real question is why she never mentioned him. And why did she want my man and family if she had a so called fiancé. I smell a rat.

"I can dig that, she didn't want her family to know that she was going to be a surrogate so she was trying to keep a low profile. She pretty much always kept to herself."

"I'm sorry but we really have to move this along sir," The officer said as he directed Dorian to the door.

"I'm sorry but I have to go."

"It's ok, nice to meet you Dorian," I replied.

Damn! So he knew who we were! I wonder just how much she told him about us? About me?

Smelling A Rat

"I'm telling you I don't trust his ass!"

"What the hell you talking about Pebbles? Damn don't we have enough shit on our minds already without you being suspicious of Fallyn's fiancé? Hell I can't even enjoy the fact that I'm bringing my son home today because of this bullshit." Adrian frowned and glanced in the rearview mirror at his son sleeping comfortably in his infant seat.

"Think about it, why else wouldn't she bring him up to us? It's because the nigga was probably going upside her head! That nigga did that shit to Fallyn! We should really think about sharing this with detective Bridges."

This was the perfect opportunity to set this shady ass nigga up. I mean who better to blame than her supposed fiancé?

"Share what with him? There you go jumping to conclusions. We don't know a damn thing about that man. You need to mind your damn business and worry about taking care of our son."

"Adrian I can't believe you gon' let this thing just slide right off your back? What if the same person who killed Fallyn decides they want us dead also?"

"Then I'll worry about it when the time comes. Hell she was living right under our roof. If they would have wanted us they knew where to find us. Like I said before this ain't none of our damn business. My only concern right now is that life in that back seat, and it should be yours as well."

"You think I'm not worried and concerned about AJ? That's my heart right there. I just can't believe you ignoring signs that are right under your damn nose."

"I ain't ignoring shit right now but yo' ass! I got too much shit on my damn mind right now to go there with you tonight Pebbles."

Look at this ungrateful son of a bitch sitting right here. I done walked through hell and back for his punk ass and this is how he talks to me? His wife? Just a damn total disregard for my feelings… I don't know what hurt me worse, the fact that Adrian wasn't buying what I was selling and the way he stood his ground on the subject of Dorian. I might have to come to grips with the fact that I didn't have the spell power over him that I once had. There use to be a time my baby would never talk to me like that. Now look at his ass. Snapping at me and disagreeing. He's just upset right now. He'll see it my way eventually.

Missing You

The sweat poured down my face as I swallowed the lump in my throat and fought the intense urge to vomit. I damn near killed myself and everyone else who was driving around me as I recklessly ran the red light and streaked through the intersection. I was shocked and mortified upon learning of the death of my girl Fallyn. And to see her disfigured body lying there on that table was unreal. And to make matters worse I had an up close and personal encounter with her murderer.

My name is Dorian Phillips and I have had a crush on Fallyn since I first laid eyes on her in high school. Unfortunately she slipped me into the friend zone and I have never seemed to find my way out. Despite the fact that we never got together she and I remained very close friends. I was always there when she needed me and vice versa. That included keeping the fact that she was going to become a surrogate from her family. She didn't always get along with her parents due to the fact that she felt like they were always too judgmental of her free spirit. As far as the rest of her relatives were concerned, they could give a damn about anyone or anything unless they were getting something out of the deal. The only person Fallyn was close to was her grandmother, however she knew that granny's old school ways wouldn't allow the flexibility of even entertaining the thought of her grandbaby having someone else's child. I can't say that I disagreed with her. I loved Fallyn and would do anything for her. It's not like she had to take this gig but she insisted hustling for her own loot. I can respect her for that but she knows I had her back if she needed me financially or otherwise.

"I told her not to do this shit!" I screamed as I shot into the parking lot of Sanders, a local hole in the wall bar that I would hit up whenever I needed to take a load off. I sat in the back at a dimly lit booth to conceal my tears. After I ordered myself two double shots of Patron I opened the photos on my cell phone to the pictures of Fallyn. I was so choked up that I had to go to the restroom to compose myself.

The part that pissed me off worse than the fact that she had been mutilated by that bitch Pebbles was the fact this all could have been avoided, granted, as I said before there is nothing wrong with becoming a surrogate for a couple in need. However this shit was bound to end on a sour note before it even got started. Long before Fallyn actually accepted the job she had come to me with some very disturbing photos. They were of someone dressed in all black murdering a woman coming out of her side door. There were also pictures of the person whom we later found out to be Pebbles aka Peyton going about her daily routine as if nothing ever happened.

I guess you could say that I was a damn fool in love because I should have used better judgment and sent the pictures to the police the day my investigation proved that Pebbles was not only living a double life, she was responsible for the murder of her husband's sister, Tasha.

I knew the incredible risk that Fallyn was taking by taking this job. And I also realized deep in my heart that she was no better than Pebbles herself for trying to blackmail her instead of going to the police. I can only imagine how that woman's poor family suffered. Now as luck would have it her family is now suffering the same fate. Fallyn always warned me that if something happened to her it most likely was from Pebbles.

I kick myself every day for being a fucking idiot and stupidly loyal to a dumb ass decision. Yes what Fallyn did was stupid, but I have to own up to the fact that not only could her murder have been prevented; Pebbles would be serving time right now. Not only that, at least Tasha's family would have some kind of closure.

As I slammed down my second shot my mind pondered the idea of going to the FBI and telling them everything. Hell I had just looked a fucking cold blooded killer in the face and shook her hand. That shit was terrifying to say the least. I had to think quickly to come up with the lie about being her fiancé. I'm not even sure if they bought it. The truth is I don't really care.

The way I saw it was, I was faced with three options, I could confront Pebbles face to face and risk being another one of her victims, I could tell the FBI but then I could be charged with concealing evidence. And a nigga like me ain't trying to go to jail. The last option would be to find a way to expose the truth to her family and the police without them knowing it was me. Lord knows I wouldn't be able to look them in the face and tell them that I knew all along Fallyn had embarked on some shit that put her in this situation.

At the end of the day I didn't sign up for this shit. I'm used to women hiring me to catch their man cheating or maybe putting the halt on an illegal check cashing ring, never any hardcore shit like this. I don't know what the hell I'm going to do now.

Haters Gon' Hate

Three months later

"Damn he look just like me when I was a baby! Wassup lil man?" Peyton exclaimed. The boldness in his tone startled the infant and he began crying.

"Dammit Peyton! Now look what you done did. You done scared my baby! It's ok boo momma is right here."

I picked up my little bundle of joy and cradled him in my arms. He settled right down when my voice switched back to its normal tone He appeared to have confused look on his little face from hearing two voices come from his momma's mouth.

This had to be the most beautiful baby I had ever seen in my entire life. And I wasn't just saying that because he was mine. He was like a Nubian Prince just waiting to be crowned king. Before I knew it I had lifted my baby in the air like Kizzy in Roots.

"Behold the first born son of Pebbles, the baddest bitch to ever walk the face of the earth. May you carry on the legacy of baddest the muthafucka that ever lived!"

"You sick as hell, you know that right?"

"Fuck off Peyton! You done made him cry again!"

Now that I had finally gotten rid of Fallyn my family was complete. The next order of business was to find a way to stop Peyton's ass from showing up unannounced. Adrian was due home from work at any moment and Lord knows we didn't need a repeat of that last incident.

All of that was neither here nor there when it came to my new found love. The fairytale was now complete. I had my man, my home, my baby, and best of all not a worry in the world now that Fallyn was gone. This was a cause for celebration.

I kissed AJ on the forehead and gently placed him in his crib. "Time to take a nap little one. Momma 'bout to turn up."

I poured myself up a tall glass of Moscato and fired up a blunt.

"Started from the bottom now we here! Started from the bottom now Pebble's team winning bitches! Started from the bottom now we here."

"This is my fucking jam! I love Drake!" I blasted the music before I took a long toke off my blunt as I Crip walked around AJ's crib.

I was thoroughly enjoying myself before Adrian walked in and blew my high.

"Pebbles! What the hell is wrong with you? Why you smoking in front of the baby? And turn this shit off! A woman done lost her life and you up in here acting like you in the damn club!"

He was livid. Before I knew it he had not only turned off my music but he actually had the nerve to walk over to me snatch the blunt right outta my hand and place it in a glass of water that was sitting on the dresser.

"I can't believe this shit right here. You done completely lost yo' damn mind. Once upon a time I thought I was married to a classy lady but I'm starting to second guess that shit! I know one damn thing you ain't about to fuck up my baby's lungs smoking that shit around him." He glared at me as he picked up AJ from his crib and took him in our room.

"Well damn! Good day to you too!" This nigga had pissed me off to the upmost! Who the hell was he to question how I raised our child. Hell a little smoke from the gangster neva' hurt anybody. If anything it was gonna help his little ass sleep tonight. And he was killing me slowly with this shit about a woman just died, like that was any of my damn concern. If I wasn't worried about her damn death why the fuck was he?

"I mean the shit was tragic and all but damn can we at least enjoy this time with our son without thinking about negative shit!" I barked.

"That some cold shit right there. I don't know who the hell I married. The Pebbles I knew, or should I say THOUGHT I knew was caring and compassionate. Now it seems like you don't give a damn about nobody but yourself. I'm starting to see yo' ass in a whole other light and the truth is that shit is ugly as hell."

"I swear I can never just BE HAPPY" I vented as my eyes began to well up. I love you and AJ so much that I would give my life for either one of you but somehow I done manage to fuck this up."

"You ain't fucked nothing up, you just need to be more aware of the foul shit that comes outta your mouth sometimes. And as far as the getting high around my son; that shit ain't even up for discussion. You his momma so start acting like it and grow yo' ass up."

I had learned from experience that there was no reasoning with him once he was at this point. I may as well chill out and let him enjoy his time with AJ before I cussed his ass clean out. Since he tried to burst my bubble I decided to take my little celebration elsewhere. I grabbed my drink, another blunt and headed to the bathroom to take a soak. Fuck it, he wanna play daddy go right ahead. I needed a break anyway. Before I knew it I would be back to work.

No Where To Hide

As the steam rose from my body my mind started to wander as I relaxed. The past three months had been such a whirl wind that I had almost put the thought of Dorian out of my mind. For the life of me I couldn't figure out why he would just lie about being Fallyn's fiancé. I tried to give the nigga the benefit of the doubt but that bitch's thirst was unquenchable when it came to my man so I know she couldn't have one of her own, or at least one that she gave a damn about. Hell maybe she was scamming his ass also. All I know is I'm getting to the bottom of this shit. When Adrian takes his ass to sleep tonight imma do me some snooping in the rest of her shit that I had hid.

Later that night

"Now lemme see what kind of damn connection this Dorian dude has to Fallyn" I said as I started scrolling through her cell phone. Luckily I remembered to take the gps tracking off of this shit. Because when it was all said and done I know the FBI done put all kind of tracers on this bitch.

"Where you at Mr. Dorian?"

I touched the screen where her contacts were. If in fact this was her man he shouldn't be that hard to find.

"Bingo! I found his ass!"

My mind could barely comprehend what I was reading as my eyes darted across the screen with lightning speed.

"Shut the hell up!"

No wonder his ass looked like a damn deer in headlights when I shook his hand at the hospital. Dorian wasn't her fiancé. He was the damn private detective friend that she told me about. And all this time I thought her ass was bluffing. Just goes to show you can never underestimate anybody. I still wouldn't have believed it if I didn't see the evidence right here in front of my own two eyes. This made perfect sense. That's why he was at the hospital. The texts in her phone perfectly coincided with what she told me about how she was going to warn him that if anything was to happen to her he was supposed to take the pictures to the police and expose my lies to everyone.

"Ok I'll give you a point for that one bitch," I laughed to myself. Now the next question was why hadn't he done it yet? What was holding him back? Unless…. he had something to hide his damn self. The more I thought about it the angrier I got. Who did this little pussy ass nigga think he was? I decided that I would sneak out the house later and place a call to Mr. Man. He may as well know upfront who he was dealing with. I could see the fear in that nigga's eyes, he wasn't 'bout that life. I mean at the end of the day imma still try to hold my shit down like any real woman would but make no mistake a bitch will jump ship if it gets too damn hot in the kitchen.

"These niggas don't know me," I laughed as I eased the side door shut and quietly walked around the block. I didn't want to risk waking Adrian up by starting the car so I took off on foot.

Once I perched myself on the monkey bars at the elementary school playground around the corner I pulled out Fallyn's phone and found Dorian's number. I decided to call him from the boost mobile number that I called momma from to keep her from tracking me down. Not only didn't I want to leave a trace, his ass might not even answer if he saw Fallyn's number.

"Watch me creep into this nigga's dream like his worst nightmare," I sneered as I dialed the number and waited for it to ring.

Meanwhile at Dorian's house

"Who the hell was this calling me at this damn hour?"

I was pissed when the phone rang. It had broken the only rest I had gotten in days. Since Fallyn's death sleep was nonexistent. Besides that my ass was on high alert, all jittery and shit just thinking about Pebble's crazy ass. I couldn't lay my head down without listening to every creaking noise, wondering if her ass done finally figured out who I was and where I lived.

"Hello"

"Boo muthafucka!"

"Who the hell is this?"

"It's Pebbles, you surprised?"

I almost pissed my damn pajama pants. My worst fear had come true. What the hell was this sicko calling me for?

"How did you get my damn number?" I snapped.

Before I knew it this bitch's voice had changed, it almost sounded like a nigga was on the other end.

"Don't toy with me muthafucka!" the voice on the other end of the line shouted. "You know damn well how I got yo' number and why I'm calling."

My heart damn near thumped out of my chest as I crept out of the bed and pulled my 45 out of my top dresser drawer. I tripped over a pair of shoes in the process and stubbed my toe on the bedframe.

"Ouch! Look I don't know what the fuck you talking about but if you got beef with me spill it."

"Shut yo' bitch ass up, trying to sound tough. Know you ain't gon' do shit. I got yo' ass running scared falling all over shit."

"Say what's on yo' mind before I hang up this damn phone!"

I tried my damndest to sound hard but she read right through that shit. The truth was I was a bitch assed nigga for letting this shit go on for as long as it had. Not only that, I was ducking and dodging, looking over my shoulder for this freaky ass muthafucka at every turn.

"Lemme just cut to the chase, yo' ass betta' think twice, betta' yet three times before trying to expose some shit on me. You never know where imma be nigga."

My legs trembled as I looked out the peephole in my front door while cocking my pistol. I dropped down to the floor and crawled on my belly to the dining room. I wasn't going down without a fight. If this crazy ass nigga wanted to bring it to my home he was about to be eating some hot lead.

"Is that a threat nigga? Well how about this? Fuck you! Peyton, Pebbles, whoever the fuck you is. You killed my girl and Adrian's sister's but if you run yo' ass up in here I got something waiting for you."

"Nigga I'm like lighting! You never know when imma strike! Trying to boss up and shit! Make no mistake bro', my balls been cut and they still bigger than yours. And while you talking that "yo' woman" shit you need to know that ya' lil hoe was after my man. That's right she played yo' simple ass!"

I couldn't believe how manly this bitch sounded; it was like someone else had taken over her body.

"That's some bullshit! The only reason Fallyn was up in that house with yo' crazy ass was to have that baby and make some extra cash then bounce. Why would she want yo' man when she had one right here waiting for her once she dropped that load?"

"Because she needed yo' gullible ass to work for her. Y'all might go way back but if she wanted you how come y'all wasn't together? Check yo' phone nigga, I'm sending you the screen shots of everything she wrote in that journal of hers about how she was gon' take my man and my baby AND live in my house. Not only that, she THOUGHT she was gon' blackmail me and get paid in the process.

"You can save all that shit for somebody who's buying it. I got enough evidence to put yo' ass under the jail."

I was going toe to toe with this shemale; all the while I was paranoid as hell. I was nervously looking out of windows and shit just in case she tried to catch me off guard.

"You feel froggy then leap nigga, but you betta' sleep with yo' finger on the trigger. Don't be no fool, tryna to be captain save a hoe. Walk away nigga. You saw my handy work. Fuck with me and you won't have no damn fingers. I'll have you wiping yo' ass with a stomp. I'm looking at yo' ass right now nigga. You look scared as hell.

Just then I jumped outta my skin when I heard a loud bang at my back door.

"AHHHHH!!!! YOU DON'T SCARE ME BITCH!!!" I screamed as I emptied the clip into door.

Tears flooded my eyes as I sat on the kitchen floor frozen while the voice on the other end of the line laughed like Vincent Price.

"Sweet dreams Dorian. Watch ya' back nigga."

After that I heard a click, she was gone. The wind continued to slam the screen on the back door despite the rounds I had just pumped in it. There was no getting around it, Pebbles must be stopped.

"Fuck it! Tomorrow I'm exposing her ass and let the chips fall where they may."

Put That Ass On Blast

I sat up half the night trying to figure out how I was going to drop the dime on this he/she without the shit being traced back to me. The police had questioned me extensively and each time I told them that I didn't know jack, all because my punk ass was scared of going to jail for harboring evidence. This is a mistake that would haunt me the rest of my life. Fallyn's blood was calling out from the grave. Knowing her the way that I did I know her soul won't rest till Pebbles got what's coming to her. As of now I wasn't considered a suspect and I wanted to keep it that way.

That shit that went down last night had me shook. Not only did I replace both doors, I set up an appointment to also beef up my security system. Thank God I lived in the hood and gun fire was the norm. Otherwise this place would have been swarming with police.

At the end of the day I couldn't run scared the rest of my damn life. My anger and hatred for this monster ran so deep that I contemplated taking care of her myself. I wanted that bitch to get a taste of her own medicine. That was until I realized that it took sick and twisted individual to kill someone in cold blood and not look back. When it was all said and done I knew in my heart that I wasn't capable of killing another human being, especially one as loony as Pebbles. She displayed all the characteristic of a typical sociopath. She was extremely dangerous and not to be toyed with. This was the game Fallyn played and lost. I also knew that if she would go as far as calling me to let me know that she was on to me it would only be a matter of time before I was next on her list.

The next day

My hands trembled as I dialed the hotline for **Hoodz Most Wanted**. I had already driven across the state line in hopes of the call not being traced back to my home. The plan was simple. Even though Pebbles was not wanted she would be in a matter of hours. By the time the network got a hold of all the pictures that I was about to scan and send to them, along with screen shots of the texts she sent me with the confession of killing Fallyn, they would be on her ass like stink on shit. Pebbles had already taken two lives in her fatal obsession with

Adrian and there would be more to follow as the walls closed in on her.

I even entertained the thought of telling Adrian personally and letting him deal with that nut case. But the truth of the matter was that after I got my head together I actually looked at the texts of the screenshots that showed Fallyn's plan to be with him and how she was scheming to not only blackmail Pebbles but to take her man also. I guess you could say that pride got the best of me and I couldn't bring myself to call the man that the woman I loved wanted. Not only that, Adrian would be out for blood once he realized how long I knew about Pebbles being a man and about her killing Tasha and not saying anything. At the end of the day it was best that I leave him alone also.

I didn't want to believe it, but the proof was right there in front of my face. As crazy as Pebbles was somehow I had the sinking feeling that this was a rare occasion that she was telling the truth and my gut has never led me wrong. Not only did the handwriting match Falynn's perfectly, it made perfect sense as to why she would always blow me off one minute but seemed to always find me when she needed something. She kept me hanging on with empty promises that we would be together one day. The excuse was always the same. She was hell bent on getting her grind on without the help of a man; at least that's what she told me. It was always "as soon as I finish this gig it's you and me." It was all lies. Now that I think back she really knew how much I loved her and used it to her advantage to get whatever she needed. She knew she had found a fool.

All this time I was thinking that the only reason Pebbles killed Fallyn was because she knew about Tasha's murder. That was only part of it; the real reason was because she wanted Adrian for herself. This explains why Pebbles worked her over so bad. It was a true crime of passion. If it had of been just about Tasha she would most likely busted a cap in her ass and called it a day.

I will always love Fallyn despite knowing what went down and how she played me, but at the end of the day it has made me look at her in a whole new light. Once upon a time I would have walked though flames with gasoline drawers on for that woman but now I can do nothing but walk away. For Fallyn and Tasha's sake I will expose Pebbles simply because she's needs to be brought to justice. That bitch needs to rot in jail. Death was too good for her.

Feeling Myself

I had to laugh in spite of myself at how smooth the transition went from having a bird that threatened to take everything I loved in my home, to me just having my little family. My man and my baby were all that I needed. There was nothing else a woman could ask for. I had successfully gotten rid of that Dorian dude and his lil dumb hoe. I will admit that he had me scared for a minute. I thought he was going to drop a dime on me, but once I realized how much of a punk bitch he really was I knew that it wouldn't take much convincing. Especially once he realized that Fallyn never wanted him. I giggled to myself when I thought about how I scared the shit out of his ass that night. I even had the fool believing I could see his bitch ass. I guess I shouldn't be too surprised. I mean I am a bad bitch when I'm on my shit.

I had also gotten my panic attacks under control and Peyton wasn't showing his ass up nearly as often. That was the only logical reason I could come up with why he surfaced in the first place. I have been under an enormous amount of stress trying to keep this lie alive and the pressure had proved to be too much. At one point I thought I was losing my damn mind, but that was all water under the bridge now.

I know that I'm still not totally out of the woods. The police are still on the hunt for Fallyn's killer and Adrian will forever pine over his sister's death and continue to work with them on that front. It's just something that I'm going to have to deal with as long as we are together. None the less I still had my backup plan thanks to the Doc. For some reason he hasn't been bothering me as much lately either. I think he finally realized that we can never be together but will always remain close friends. And one thing is for certain, no matter what happens the Doc had my back. He also knew that I would pay him back every red cent I owed him once I got the chance.

The real icing on the cake was the fact that Adrian's parents had not only met me a while back and didn't have a clue of my real identity; they also fell completely in love with their grandson. Even though these weren't my parents it did somehow give me some kind of fulfillment seeing as my parents had yet to see him. I will admit it was kind of hard at first to smile in their face, all the while knowing I had killed their daughter and my best friend. I soon got over it when I saw how much of a big happy family we had become. This was further reinforcement that I had made the right decision.

Adrian and I still had trust issues to work on in our marriage from the time when Peyton showed his punk ass up and ruined everything. However we were slowly working it out. The baby had brought a joy to our life that was unspeakable.

Busted

It was a lazy Sunday evening. I had just gotten out of the shower and slipped into a cute outfit and styled my hair. My boo was taking me and the baby out to dinner and I wanted to look my best. While I was in the guest bathroom giving myself a final once over I overheard the TV in the living room. It was tuned into **Hoodz Most Wanted.** I dropped the hand held mirror I was holding and let it shatter to the floor when I heard them say Pebbles aka Peyton! I was mortified! I quickly peeped into the room to see if Adrian was there. Thank God he wasn't! I had to turn that shit off with the quickness and get his ass out of the house. Just as I was about to enter the room he suddenly appeared with a beer in his hand and took a seat. If I could have died at that very moment I would have. My cover had been blown! It terrified me to think about what Adrian would do when he found out that not only was I a man but also a murderer. I stood and watched for a split second as his mouth fell open from the shock of seeing my image on the screen next to Peyton's. I knew it would only be a matter of minutes before he would come looking for me so there was no time to waste.

My hands shook violently as I quickly went to AJ's room and bundled him up. I tipped out of the side door and secured him in his car seat. This was it. The gig was finally up and I had no choice but to resort to my backup plan. Luckily I already had everything I needed pack in my getaway ride for both of us. The only thing I needed to do was get to it. I knew it was only going to be a matter of time before the cops would have this place surrounded. I'm surprised they didn't already. I needed to strike while the irons were hot! And the time was now. Adrian could either go along like he had some damn sense and let me explain along the way or I would have to take his ass with force.

I quickly recovered the box of weapons of Fallyn's that I had hidden in the garage just in case I needed them and slipped them in the trunk, but not before slipping the taser under my shirt and tucking it in my jeans. The only thing left to do now was to run back in to grab my purse. I immediately broke out on a cold sweat upon reaching the living room and not seeing Adrian. Where the hell was he? Just as I was about to turn and head to our room I was met with a right hook to my jaw. This nigga had stole me! My body hit the floor with a thud. He had hit me so hard that I thought I was going to black out from the pain. I looked up to see Adrian glaring down at me with the most hateful stare one person could ever give another.

"Who the fuck are you nigga?"

Adrian had completely lost it. He was in an unmitigated rage and there was no stopping him. His jaw was clenched and his eyes were bulging out of his head. I tried to sit up and scoot up against the wall to brace myself but his fury knew no bounds.

"Wait, please lemme expla……"

I couldn't even finish the word before he launched a full-fledged attack upon me. Before I knew it I was being stomped repeatedly. His nostrils flared each time his foot connected with my ribs, causing me to retreat to the fetal position.

"Imma kill you muthafucka! You killed Tasha!"

I rolled out of the way just in time to avoid his boot coming down on my head. I was hurt and humiliated. I couldn't believe that after I all I had went through and sacrificed to be with this nigga he would turn on me like this. The fact that he had caught me off guard and was trying to do great bodily harm to my ass was over shadowed by my own anger. My manly strength had now remerged and I was back on my feet.

Adrian tried to rush me and was met with an upper cut.

"Nigga I told yo' ass the first time to keep yo' hands to yoself!" Peyton yelled.

Adrian lunged at me once again, this time landing on top of me as we crashed into the glass cocktail table. "Where the fuck is my son?"

I quickly kicked him off of me and pulled out the taser. As he tried to stagger back to his feet I shoved it right between his ass cheeks and gave him a full blast! He foamed at the mouth and pissed himself as the current ripped through his body.

"Now look what you made me do!" I cried.

I didn't want to hurt my boo but there was no reasoning with him. I quickly drug his limp body to the kitchen and duck taped his mouth shut before taping his hands together. I peered out of the side door to see if there was anyone outside before pushing him out and forcing him into the car. I checked for on lookers before pulling out of the driveway and speeding off.

Death Ride

Before heading for the highway I peeped at AJ one last time, making sure he was secure. This was about to be a wild ass ride. Thank goodness my baby was fast asleep. It was evident that I was gon' have to fuck his daddy up but I didn't want my baby being knocked around in all the commotion. That's what a real momma does; worry about safety first. This was yet another reason I knew that I should have been born a woman. My maternal instincts were stronger than ever.

"Wake yo' ass up nigga!" I yelled as I slapped Adrian upside his head. His head rocked back and forth as he slowly came to. Once he was fully wake and realized what was happening he started kicking violently and twisting in his seat.

I pulled the taser out and showed it to him as a reminder of what would be in store for his ass if he didn't cooperate. When he finally settle down I could see him staring in the rearview mirror at little AJ as he began to weep.

"Don't cry now nigga!" Peyton yelled. "You should have loved me just the way I was and none of this shit would be happening! What about all the tears I shed for you?"

Adrian responded by banging his head against the headrest in disagreement.

I was in such a frenzy that I rapidly switched between myself and Peyton with ease.

"Do you know how much I sacrificed to love you? Do you?" I asked slapping him in the head with the taser.

"All the shit I had done to my body. All these fucking clothes, the wigs, the lies… I didn't want to kill Tasha she was like a sister to me too but she threatened to tell you everything and I couldn't let that happen. Then Fallyn thought her stupid ass was gon' run up and take my place with you and so I had to kill again. I only did for us, I did it for love."

I don't think he heard a word of anything past the point of my confession of killing Tasha. He appeared to be in a state of shock staring out of the window.

"You listening to me punk?" Peyton barked. "I said I loved yo' bitch ass! I've loved yo' ass ever since we was kids! But naw! You didn't want anything to do with me as a man so I had to resort to this. You made me do this!"

I mashed the pedal to the floor as I swerved off the highway into a dirt road that led to the spot with my getaway car. Little AJ's car seat jerked back and forth as we bounced along the rocky pavement. Pretty soon Adrian started looking at the wooded environment around us as though he was trying to figure out where we were.

"Ain't looking too good for you is it nigga?" Peyton asked as we pulled up to the spot where the car was parked and turned off the engine. "Ain't noooobody gon' find us here."

The light was fading as dusk rapidly approached. The woods were eerily quiet and the only sounds that could be heard were the branches creaking and leaves crackling underfoot as I exited the car and popped the trunk. After retrieving the gun from Fallyn's trick box I opened the door to the passenger side and placed the barrel against Adrian's temple.

"Step out the car nicely for me bae."

I could see the horror in his eyes as he contemplated his demise. Once he was out of the vehicle I yanked him a few feet away from the car and busted him in the head with the butt of the pistol.

"Get on yo' damn knees!"

Once I forced him to the ground I stood in front of him and pointed the gun to his head. My heart damn near thumped out of my chest as I was now faced with killing the man that I loved.

"I love you sooo much Adrian. And I know you still love me. Just say it…. and we can be together forever. We can run away from all this bullshit and continue on with our lives."

It hurt me so bad to see my baby on the ground broken and defeated. But I knew he would never forgive me for killing Tasha. Nor would he accept the fact that I was once a man. Personally I didn't see what the big damn deal was if he loved me before he knew the truth he should love me now. All he would have to do was say the word and I would be his forever. I decided to give him one last chance to declare his love for me and to beg for my forgiveness for all the shit that he had put me through.

"Just say you still love me Adrian" I said as I pulled the tape from his mouth to let him speak.

"I will never love you! As a matter of fact I hate yo' ass! Gimme my son and let us go you fucking sicko!"

I was appalled and taken aback. The nerve of this muthafucka! I had never had such hateful words spoken to me in my entire life.

Before I had a chance to respond Adrian attempted to stand to his feet. I quickly thwarted his efforts by shooting him in his right kneecap.

"Ahhhhh!!" He screamed out in agony as he fell to the ground.

"Oh so it's like that? You hate me? Pebbles, the woman who loved you from day one?"

"Fuck you in the asshole you faggot son of a bitch! I hope yo' ass burns to a crisp in hell, I would gladly watch," he grunted as he writhed around in pain unable to grab his knee due to his hands being bound.

My pain had now turned to fury.

"Oh so that's what you think of me after all I done sacrificed for you? I'm a faggot son of a bitch that you want to watch burn? Is that what you think of the mother of your child? Well I'm sorry that you are so unhappy. Allow me to take yo' bitch ass out of yo' misery!"

I walked back over to the car and pulled a two by four from the trunk. Adrian caught a glimpse of the punishment that was in store for him and made one last attempt to rise to his feet. I decided to humor myself and let him hobble along on one leg before approaching him and kicking his good leg out from under him.

"Not too bad for a faggot huh?" Peyton sneered before cracking the board across his shoulder.

His screams echoed in the silent darkness that had now fell upon us. I turned on the car lights before continuing my brutal assault.

Adrian's body flailed about on the ground as the two by four met his flesh over and over again, leaving him faced down squirming and squealing in the dirt. I flipped him over to see his lungs still struggling to find life.

"You sorry piece of shit!" I yelled as my foot connected with his face causing him to spit out teeth. "What you got to say now?"

He gulped for air, searching for enough oxygen to speak. "Fuck you Peyton" he managed to let out in a weak whisper.

I slammed down the two by four once again, this time connecting with his skull. It was lights out.... I quickly dragged his limp lifeless body to the edge of the foothill and kicked it over.

After replacing all the items in the trunk I fed and changed AJ, switched cars, dressed in one of my disguises and drove off.

I picked up the phone and called the Doc. I knew that this shit was all over the news by now and I wanted to let him know that I was ok.

"Hello!"

The excitement in his voice from seeing an unknown number was evident that he had a feeling that it was me. I never spoke a word. Instead I just listened to his voice.

"Hello, hello who is this?"

I continued to sit quietly on the other end. Pretty soon the Doc began to sniffle.

"Is this you hoofy?" he managed to choke out.

I never answered; instead I let out a deep sigh that responded for me.

"I will always love you Pebbles, no matter what happens. Take care of yourself."

I hung up the phone and continued on my journey to nowhere. The tears rolled down my cheeks as I replayed all the beautiful memories Adrian and I shared together. If given the chance to do things differently I wouldn't change a damn thing. You know the saying.

It's better to have loved and lost than to have never loved at all. This rang beyond true for me, at least I can say that once in my lifetime I found and had my one true love. How many of you bitches can actually say that? Think about that before you try to judge me.

Left For Dead

In the pitch blackness I opened my eyes to look up at a blanket of stars. I was freezing and in excruciating pain, unable to move. That's when it hit me; Pebbles tried to kill me.

"Imma kill that bastard."

The End

Midnite Love

Made in the USA
Lexington, KY
17 July 2016